SECURITY DIRECTORATE DOSSIERS

VOLUME 2

Also by Alexandria Blaelock

SHORT STORY COLLECTIONS
The Histories of Hayward Hall
Lovelorn, Lovestruck and Love at First Sight
Common or Garden Variety Heroes
Case Files of the Wilkinson Detective Agency
Unavoidable Fates
Christmas Travesties
Five Faces of Felicia Clarke
Little Place Called Home
Security Directorate Dossiers volume 1

FICTION
That Love Nonsense
Taipan vs Brown
The Ghost and Ms Cox
Friends Like That

MS BLAELOCK'S BOOKS
Stress Free Dinner Parties
Signature Wardrobe Planning
Holistic Personal Finance
Minimally Viable Housekeeping
Planning a Life Worth Living

SELECTED SHORT STORIES

Alma's Grace	Ship in a Bottle
Balancing the Book	Simone Says Hands in the Air
Best Friends Forever	Special Relativity in Space
Christmas Bonanza	The Bygone Boyfriend
Christmas Conflagration	The Day the Schedule Broke
Christmas Kisses	The Ghost Detectors
Fate in Your Hands	The Kiss of Death
Long Weekend in the Snow	The Mince Pie Mystery
Love in the Past Tense	The Palace Hotel
Mystery of the Master Suite	The Pseudonym's Bride
Needy Bitch	The Shadow Thieves
Remains of Christmas	The Space Time Paradox
Secret Singer	Toy Soldiers
Shining Star	Waylon's Way

SECURITY DIRECTORATE DOSSIERS

VOLUME 2

ALEXANDRIA BLAELOCK

BlueMere Books
MELBOURNE, AUSTRALIA

Ordering Information:
Discounts are available on quantity purchases. For details, contact
orders@bluemerebooks.com.

Security Directorate Dossiers volume 2/Alexandria Blaelock
hardback ISBN: 978-1-922744-78-4
paperback ISBN: 978-1-922744-79-1
digital ISBN: 978-1-922744-80-7
AI generated audio: 978-1-922744-81-4

Book Layout © BookDesignTemplates.com
Cover Art
Security Directorate Dossiers v2 © grandfailure /Depositphotos
Life in the Security Directorate © Tithi Luadthong/Depositphotos
Honoris Virilis Respectu ©
i.am.norton33@gmail.com/Depositphotos
Calling it a Day © khius/Depositphotos
Veni Vidi Vici © grandfailure/Depositphotos
Pursuit of Power © grandfailure/Depositphotos

Contents

INTRODUCTION

It seems to me, my Security Directorate universe is the gift that just keeps giving.

Not for its citizens, of course, but for me who writes, and you who read the stories.

In the first volume's introduction, I explained the idea came out of World War II documentaries and the Syrian Civil War (not that it's over).

And I explained a little behind the inspiration for a Genomics Bureau that *literally* controls births, deaths and marriages, and an Office of Public Enlightenment to interpret the truth for its citizens.

I still find the potential applications of eugenics, and the complementary policies of genocide and breeding control ghoulishly fascinating.

Not to mention the recent attempts by certain governments to control the truth, so an Office of Enlightenment looks like a good way for a fascist state to buy itself the time and space to grow and develop as a country.

Especially with departments for internal, as well as external truths.

All in all, regardless of who's in charge, a fair amount of population control requires having the right people in the right places to ensure compliance.

Not to mention a casually ruthless disregard for its citizens.

I worry a little that makes me some kind of egregious monster.

But when I read books by other authors in similar veins, I'm reassured we all need these fictions to help us see where such policies could end up.

After all, we writers are good at following these thoughts to their logical conclusions.

So, here are some more speculative stories about life in the Security Directorate.

This time, we're looking more at the mid-level officers who undertake this work. The perils of getting up and going to work every day.

Their choices, for better or worse, and how the consequences play out.

- In *Life in the Security Directorate*, Eve struggles to come to terms with life in the Directorate, and finds her own way out.
- While *Honoris Virilis Respectu* shows Major General John Simm struggling with the difference between his version of the truth and the Director General's.
- Potentially, Captain Maeryn Prothero is on the wrong side of the Directorate in *Calling it a Day*.
- Moving on, in *Veni Vidi Vici*, Second Lieutenant Cora Meadows must make a one woman assault on her own Exploratorem Station.

- And finally, in *Pursuit of Power*, Captain Tara Cline pursues a serial killer with a dirty secret.

Every day I sit down after tea and watch the tv news. The international reports show me there's a lot of Security Directorate-like activity going on out there.

In some cases, it's a little more frightening than I've imagined up to now.

I look forward to seeing how this affects the Security Directorate, and I hope you do too.

Alexandria Blaelock
Melbourne, Australia
November, 2023

ALEXANDRIA BLAELOCK

AUTHOR OF FATE IN YOUR HANDS

LIFE IN THE SECURITY DIRECTORATE

A SECURITY DIRECTORATE SHORT STORY

LIFE IN THE SECURITY DIRECTORATE

Eve closed her eyes and leaned her forehead against the stationery cupboard door. Most of her days were pretty shitty, but for some reason, this one was shittier than most.

Maybe not the shittiest day of her life, that was probably the day she'd been born.

After she passed the Genomics Bureau postnatal testing, her parents had quickly signed her and all her rights over to the State. She was remanded to the State Academy of Cultural Regulation while her parents tried to live down the shame of producing what was colloquially known as a superhero.

She took a deep calming breath.

What was it she needed right now?

Black Earl Grey tea with a thin slice of lemon. And a lemon shortbread biscuit to go with it. In a nice vintage, rose-patterned bone china cup and saucer.

She pulled the cupboard door open, and there it was, steaming gently on top of a stack of notebooks.

She smoothed a few stray mouse-brown loose hairs back into her long ponytail and took her tea back to her desk.

Kicking off her sensible shoes, she pulled open the bottom drawer of her broken pedestal unit, pulled out a small cushion which she placed on her desk and propped her feet up on it.

Drawing the silence around her like a cloak of invisibility, she closed her eyes and inhaled the tea's citrus aroma before taking a sip.

Designated FX-84325, she'd been given all the love and care you'd expect of a State-run Academy - bullying, intensive education, hard physical work, mind control and so on.

Instead of being trained to fit in, the children were intensively trained to stand out. At least they were if they didn't die during basic training.

Survivors had no choice but to join the Protection Squadron. The terrifyingly impassive guardians of whatever the State named the public good.

No friends or family to influence their rigid, unbiased and unthinking law enforcement.

During the fiercely competitive initial training, she hadn't displayed a useful skill, like reading or influencing minds, blowing up or moving heavy loads or getting places really fast.

Subsequently, she'd been redesignated FG-84325, and shunted into general training for low-level operatives; colloquially known as goons.

She rotated her shoulders a few times and rocked her head back and forth across them to try and relieve the tension and stiffness.

As bad as her subsequent life had been, Eve was grateful she'd been declared faulty and expelled from the programme.

As a failed superhero, she at least had the chance of a somewhat normal life.

It wasn't easy though - the Directorate sent out undercover agents as failed superheroes too, so you were greeted with suspicion wherever you went. It was very rare anyone would trust or want to get to know you.

Now designated Eve, the State mandated name for failed female operatives, with a permanent record of attendance at superhero school, the population treated her as warily as a jaguar zoo escapee.

Not to mention that expulsion left her standing outside the school gates with just the clothes on her back.

No family, no money, no support. Presumably, given the training, the idea was to ensure you didn't survive on your own.

She dunked her biscuit in the tea and savoured the flavour as it slowly dissolved on her tongue.

Eve had always been lucky. She'd always been able to lay her hands on whatever she needed. Whether that was an extra food ration, a safe place to hide, or a helping hand. Or maybe that was her superpower.

Undetected, because she needed it to be.

For her, it was a pretty useful power to have, even though it wasn't always reliable. She wasn't sure how need was determined, or what would meet that need.

Or where the stuff came from. Or given it disappeared when she was done needing it, what happened to it.

She took a deep breath and stretched as she let it out in a sigh.

Her ability to quickly obtain required supplies with a minimum of fuss had earned her a tiny, yet private office in the warehouse.

It was gloomy, full of broken furniture and a long way from where the business action happened.

But it was all hers.

Plus, her unwavering cheerfulness in the face of constant doubt had gained her a certain amount of tolerance from her colleagues.

She would always be an outsider, but she was treated reasonably well and accepted at company functions.

Though, fearing alcohol-fuelled reprisals for Protection Squad activities, she always managed to leave before the drinking started in earnest.

She didn't know for sure, but it made sense the Squad would monitor her activities more carefully than normals, so she'd been vigilant.

In general, she lived a quiet life, skirting the fringes of other people's lives. She kept to herself, dressed and acted to avoid attention, and tried not to use her power unless it was necessary.

But she was lonely. She worked alone, then went home alone, to her tiny apartment full of smiling stuffed animals. She bought cookbooks from exotic places she would never be permitted to visit and cooked single-serve meals.

After dinner, she curled up in a blanket, reading borrowed books, living an adventurous kind of life with close friends forbidden to her.

Imagining she was allowed a boyfriend, someone to kiss and openly share her feelings with.

Today's borrowed tea and biscuit was relatively minor - a quiet moment outside of normal. Once she'd been followed into a building, and exited from another in someone else's body.

She sighed again, put the empty teacup down, and massaged her temples. Just for a moment, she imagined another life.

One where the State didn't monitor and control the people. Where there was no such thing as a Protection Squad, and people lived their lives freely and openly.

What would that be like?

Standing up, she stretched again and walked across the room to the window overlooking the warehouse. The sun was shining, birds were singing, and a warm, soft floral breeze blew through a crack in the glass.

Given the opportunity, she'd have climbed out the window to see what that other life was like, but the bars made that impossible.

For the moment she'd satisfy herself with a borrowed breath of fresh air.

The stiff office door scraped and jittered as someone tried to open it.

Eve turned away from the window and walked towards her desk. By the time she got there, the room had reverted to its usual dingy appearance.

The sunny exterior view faded to a dirty safety glass window overlooking the warehouse. The cushion, teacup and saucer also disappeared.

An odour of must rolled over the light scent of flowers.

She stepped back into her shoes, smoothed her grey pencil skirt down and kicked the pedestal drawer shut.

Then picked up a notebook covered in a girly cartoon pattern from her neat and clean desk, along with a pencil topped by a half-used rabbit eraser.

She pasted a cheerful smile on her face and was ready to take on whoever came through the door.

It suddenly gave way, and a tall, well-dressed muscular man fell through, tripping a few steps forward to collide with her.

She deftly caught and held him to stop him falling over. Trying not to inhale his brisk outdoorsy scent, she let him catch his balance.

He quickly took a step back. While it was probably for his own protection, Eve was grateful to have more air around her.

"I'm sorry, the door's sticky. I've called the maintenance department, but it's a very low priority."

He smiled and waved a hand in its direction, "there's no need. It's not your fault."

Eve smiled a small smile and bowed her head in acknowledgement.

"I'm Adam, I'm here about the Statutory Department's order for half a pallet of copy paper."

Eve looked a little more closely at him. His name labelled him a failed superhero just like her, but his clothing suggested he was an agent.

She'd never met another failure and didn't know what to expect.

She schooled her face, trying not to look too alarmed or interested. She was fairly sure she hadn't done anything to raise suspicion, but he could still be there for a random audit.

She put her notebook and pencil down and nodded professionally. "I've prepared your order for dispatch. If you'll follow me, I'll show you where it is."

She opened the warehouse door and led him down the steel stairs, his eyes boring holes in her back.

Not literally, of course, he was a failure too, but her recently relaxed shoulders started tensing up again anyway.

As they walked through the racked stock, Eve was at war with herself.

On one side, she was eaten up with curiosity about who he was and how he came to be there.

Even though she was essentially quarantined from the normals, she thought someone might have mentioned there was another failure in the building.

Or were there so many of them by now that it barely rated a mention?

On the other side, who was he, and why was he there? Was he auditing her?

Was he involved in some other State ordered action, even if he was only the copy boy? Did he know she was an Eve?

How did he fail out of the Academy?

But as they moved further away from her office, the silence lengthened. All too soon they'd reached the stacked trolley, and it was too late to ask anything at all.

Eve put her cheerful face back on and nodded her ponytailed head at the trolley, "here we are - all stacked up and ready to go. Can you manage from here?"

He gave the trolley an experimental push and smiled ruefully. "I think I'll be okay with the trolley, but I'm new here and have no idea how to get back to my workstation."

Eve nodded once, "are you on the Statutory Department floor?"

"I guess so."

"Fine, I can take you back," she gestured toward the side of the warehouse, "this way."

He took the trolley, made a small u-turn to get it going, and headed in the direction she'd pointed.

Determined not to lose this second opportunity, she stepped up and walked beside him, "have you been with us long?"

"About a week. I'm here collating some documents to send to the Office of Public Enlightenment."

"I see, do you work for Public Enlightenment?"

Adam snorted, "do you really think with the name Adam I'd be working for Public

Enlightenment? I'm just an admin temp; here to fetch coffee, sharpen pencils and do the copying."

Eve pursed her lips for a moment. He seemed very open about his failure, but other than that, it was too soon to trust him, "I understand."

"I heard there's an Eve here somewhere, do you know where I might find her?"

Eve gasped and stepped back, what did he want with an Eve?

And did he want an Eve, or did he want her?

Adam turned to look quizzically at her suddenly shuttered face.

"I am Eve, what do you want with me."

He held out in supplication, "I'm sorry, I didn't mean to scare you. I just overheard a conversation about you and wanted to meet you. I've never met another failure before."

His answer was a little too much like what she wanted to hear.

If she was an agent, it'd be the kind of thing she'd say to try and gain trust. But at the same time, it was exactly what she'd been thinking about him.

Was this her superpower trying to give her what she needed?

She frowned at him, "then you'll know that just makes you seem more like an agent than a failure. What did you overhear?"

"Essentially, that you seem so nice and normal, they can't believe you're a superhero. They were speculating that something went wrong during your postnatal testing and you'd been misdiagnosed. I've never heard anything like it before."

Eve slumped back against the racking. If, in fact, any of that was true, it was high praise from her colleagues. But could he or they really be trusted?

Her empty heart really hoped so.

She needed a chocolate, and wondering vaguely what he might need, reached hopefully into the stock behind her. She pulled out a packet and without looking at it, opened it and offered him first go.

"Oh my god, it's salted macadamias, my favourite! Where did you get them?"

That answered the question about whether she could pick up what other people needed. "I spend most of my time down here, and it's too tiresome to keep running up the stairs to the office, so I stash snacks about the place. Would you like something to drink?"

Adam smiled, "how about a delicious can of State Regulated Cola then?"

To give her story some substance, she handed over the nuts, darted out of sight round around the rack and came back with two lukewarm cans.

He laughed, clenched the nut packet between his teeth and reached for a can.

He opened it and handed it back before taking the other. "I guess your colleagues are right, you *are* too normal to be a superhero."

Eve blushed prettily and put on her cheerful face, "you're too kind. What about you, were you misdiagnosed as well?"

Going by the shock in his face, it was probably a little too intimate too soon. She took a quick gulp of the drink and came up choking.

He pounded her back to help clear her airways.

Once her coughs had subsided, she said "I'm sorry Adam, that was very presumptuous of me. Please forget I asked."

"No, it's not that," he said, sipping his drink, "it's just that like you, I'm not used to people talking to me."

He hooked a big box from the bottom rack with his foot and gestured for her to sit before snagging one for himself.

"Partway through the skills assessment, I became ill and lost my ability. The Academy tried a variety of treatments, but couldn't bring it back."

He shrugged, "after a couple of years of experimentation, I was invalided out."

It was a plausible story, but it had taken her decades of hard work to make the pitiful career progress she'd made.

How did he come to be wearing a high-quality suit working with classified information for the Office of Public Enlightenment?

She took a more careful drink. "So you work for the Security Directorate now?"

He looked at her in disbelief, "I'm sorry, I don't get how you came to that conclusion?"

Eve gestured at his suit pants, "well, you're an overly confident, fit and healthy failed superhero wearing a decent suit. Why would anyone think you were anything other than an agent?"

He snorted, "I can see why you'd think that, but I'm Adam Rochester of the Signals Department Rochesters. They didn't renounce me when I was invalided out of the Academy. Came close though."

Well, that made all the difference - rich boy from a cultural elite family with all the benefits that brought him.

"So you just get preferential treatment because your family's high up in the political hierarchy?"

"Well not entirely, the law is still the law, regardless of who your family is. I'm still Adam - I can't be a superhero, and I can't live a normal life."

He closed his eyes for a moment and took a swig from the can. "My family tolerates me, but I'm still a failure in their eyes. It just means they're compelled to take care of me, though they've made it plain they expect me to take care of myself and not drain their resources."

He smiled evilly, "I bet they regret setting up a trust fund for me as well as not renouncing me."

Eve drained her drink and left the empty can on the rack. Dare she conduct an experiment of her own?

Failed superheroes aren't permitted physical contact, but she needed to know whether he was friend or foe, so she daringly nudged his shoulder with her own.

"I sometimes wonder what it would be like to live somewhere else where these rules don't apply don't you?"

He frowned a little, but made no mention of the contact, "I can't imagine living anywhere else, but maybe more like a normal. To have friends and parties - to be welcomed, not shunned."

They sat in companionable silence, each trying to imagine a future that wasn't State controlled.

He sighed, "I've been gone a while, I suppose I should get back to my copying."

Eve echoed his sigh, she didn't think it had been that long of a break, and agent or not, she really didn't want to let him go, "it's been nice, thanks for taking the time to chat."

She stood and placed his empty nut bag and can with her own "the goods lift is this way."

He stood, dusted his hands on his pants and kicked the boxes back into their places in the rack, "do you want me to take the rubbish?"

"No thanks, I'll get rid of it when I get back."

He gave the trolley a solid push to get it moving again, and they crossed the final space to the lift.

Eve pushed the up button, "if the lift opened to a parallel universe, would you get in?"

He glanced at her, "Now who sounds like an agent?"

She laughed, "I know, but what's the worst that can happen? We get euthanised?"

"Don't you think they'd torture you for information or something before they kill you?"

"I don't know, it's not something you hear about, is it? Not knowing, and imagining is worse than knowing for sure."

The lift binged, "last chance" she shouted, "in or out?"

He opened his mouth, she wasn't sure whether it was to scream or answer her question, but the lift doors opened to reveal the padded walls of the goods lift, and it was too late.

She waited for him to manoeuvre the trolley into the carriage before entering herself and pushing the button for the 57th floor. She stood to the side, facing Adam, hands clasped in front of her.

He flinched as it shuddered and dropped slightly before starting its ascent. "Why would you even think about parallel universes?" he asked.

"I think it's the nature of all humans, superhero or normal, to seek freedom and happiness. What about you and your friends and parties? Aren't you tired of living alone?"

"I suppose. But, given I'm a Rochester, I'm never really alone. Though I get all the Rochester obligations without the benefits. It would be nice to please myself occasionally."

"Can I take that as Yes! I'll get off at the closest parallel universe?"

He jiggled the trolley as he thought, "You know what, I might be wrong, but I can't see how it could be worse than here. Aside from arriving there with nothing."

"Like the ultimate refugee - nothing to lose and everything to gain."

He laughed awkwardly, "yes, I suppose so."

The lift binged as they approached their destination, and Adam bunched his muscles, preparing to push the trolley out into the corridor.

The doors opened to reveal a lush green meadow, drenched in sunshine. Eve pushed the button that held the doors open.

The wind bent the grass, pushing the fresh scent of the open countryside into the carriage. A butterfly flew in, found no flowers and flew out again.

Adam's jaw dropped, and he rubbed his eyes as if he couldn't believe what he was seeing.

She smiled at him, "we've reached our destination. Do you want to please yourself enough to follow me?"

His once-friendly face contorted, and he snarled, "I knew you were too good to be true."

It seemed he was an undercover agent after all. He tried to get out from behind the trolley, but right now, she needed him to stay where he was, and the trolley wheels obliged.

He lunged at her as she stepped out onto the grass, but he just succeeded in dislodging boxes of paper and fencing himself in.

Perhaps he was just afraid, "this really is your last chance Adam, once the doors close, they'll reopen, and you'll be back at the Statutory Department. Neither one thing nor the other."

"I don't know what you've done to me, but there is no other universe. I'm placing you under arrest - get back in this lift."

The wind pulled her hair loose from her ponytail, and it crackled around her head like electricity.

"You know I can't do that Adam. My sad life was over the minute you entered my building. I don't know where I am, or if my power will work here. But no matter what, I'm better off here."

He snarled and lunged again.

"This really is your last chance Adam. We don't even have to stay together. You can make your own path to your future."

"There is nothing for me there that I don't have here. For all I know, it will be worse there. You'll probably be eaten by lions."

She smiled sadly, "thanks for showing me what I missed Adam. I wish you a future of freedom and happiness."

Eve didn't need an escape route, so she raised a hand in farewell, let the lift doors close with a final clunk and disappear.

She stretched and took a deep breath of fresh air. It didn't matter where she went, so she closed her eyes and spun around a few times, then started walking. She couldn't wait to see what this world had to offer.

THE END

ALEXANDRIA BLAELOCK

AUTHOR OF FATE IN YOUR HANDS

HONORIS VIRILIS RESPECTU

A SECURITY DIRECTORATE SHORT STORY

HONORIS VIRILIS RESPECTU

Major General John Simm stood at his office window looking down and out over the City.

It was a beautiful day; the sun was shining, and the glass radiated a slight warmth back to him.

Were he a fanciful man who believed in a beneficent universe, he might have believed the small touch of warmth on his face, against the air-conditioned chill at his back was a small blessing.

Or perhaps a token of gratitude for his efforts.

But he was a Security Directorate Officer.

A Eugenics Programme success, he'd passed the Genomics Bureau post-natal testing, survived the State Academy of Cultural Regulation with a useful genetic "superpower" and graduated with Honours from the University of Civilisation.

Into a career he'd more or less been bred and trained for.

Out in the City, people the size of ants walked the streets in their shirt sleeves. Uniform jackets cast aside or held by a crooked finger over the shoulder, and uniform caps set at jaunty angles on heads.

It seemed joy strolled the streets with the citizens.

Something in the sunshine gave them the hope all was well in their universe.

And it was Simm's job to make sure they believed it was.

Because if they believed all was well, then it was.

He decided where the truth lay and oversaw the teams crafting the key messages to go out in the news feed.

That his office was so high above the population was symbolic, of course; given his high rank in the Propaganda Bureau, he needed to be seen to be above the common people.

To be surrounded by untainted empty space to exercise the appropriate level of "impartial" judgement.

Not for the first time, he wished he worked in an older building, with windows that opened so he could, now and again, let fresh ideas in with the fresh air.

All this streamlined modern efficiency wasn't very helpful for choosing a way forward, regulation twenty square metre glass office or not.

He sighed and returned to the black leather chair behind his overly large mahogany desk, boot heels clicking across the white marble floor.

The desk had its back to an impressively plain mahogany bookshelf packed with red leather-bound books and campaign awards.

A green pot plant on the top added a touch of life and colour as it spilled down the side.

He sprawled as much as his rank and training would allow.

And looked past the two black leather guest chairs in front of his desk, and the matching mahogany and leather conversational setting between them and the door.

Staring at the large picture of the Director General watching over him, dominating the view from his desk.

Just in case he forgot who was really in charge of the truth.

All had been well in his universe until a few weeks ago.

Captain Evans was bringing coffee in for him and his department heads when she'd slipped on the recently refinished floor and broken her hip.

He hadn't realised how dependent on her he'd become until she was gone.

The surgery was successful, but he'd be without her for months while she undertook physical therapy.

Her attitude had been so positive he'd chosen to watch out for her. Ensure her medical needs were taken care of, and guaranteed her position within the Directorate.

But he was already facing pressure to replace her.

And it was possible she wouldn't recover her full mobility, and even though she had a desk job, this put her career in jeopardy.

No one wants to be confronted by officers wounded in the line of duty.

Not to mention, no matter how successful the recovery, she wouldn't be combat-ready for active service ever again.

In a completely random stroke of good fortune, Captain Evans was the first assistant allocated to him on his promotion to the post years ago.

Aside from being an excellent administrator, she knew a lot about him and his executive team, and he could safely rely on her to adequately progress issues on his behalf.

While she hadn't passed sufficient units to graduate from the University of Civilisation, her underprivileged background had given her street smarts in spades, and she'd been able to talk her way out of the Protection Squad and into an administrative career.

And given him good advice when he'd tested ideas on her.

Then again, maybe street smarts was the genetic "superpower" that got her through the Academy and into University.

And a field promotion to officer-status.

Not that you were permitted to discuss or compare your powers.

But hers had made her sufficiently useful, and she was allocated to him on that basis.

Plus, her cheerful disposition was a ray of sunshine in itself, making friends and allies of all she came into contact with.

Not to mention her solid work ethic had gained the respect of his colleagues and direct reports.

Or that she was a keen judge of character, and had saved his arse on more than one occasion.

Her replacement, Lieutenant Smythe, had graduated, and that was the very best you could say about him. The worst was he was perhaps so thoroughly indoctrinated he didn't seem to have a single unauthorised thought in his head.

He couldn't rely on the boy to anticipate anything, or take the initiative to progress the slightest of issues without the most detailed of explicit instructions.

Not to mention Smythe's attitude clearly communicated his disdain for the posting and his belief he deserved something better. Thus he'd taken next to no time alienating Simm's colleagues and direct reports as thoroughly as Evans had charmed them.

The brat couldn't even make a decent cup of coffee.

The only thing he had in his favour were high-ranking parents, and they could only get him so far in the face of his incompetence.

The sooner Simm was shot of him, the better.

The day Evans slipped was the day he'd quietly started questioning the propaganda, and his place in the myth-making department of the Directorate.

Every day, he swore his loyalty to the Director General, the same as every other day since he started at the Academy.

But it was becoming clear to him that his idea of what the Security Directorate was, and the current Director General's idea were not the same.

Obviously, the communications equated them quite closely, but the Directorate existed outside the person who held the position of Director General.

A concept the current incumbent did not seem to grasp.

Or want to.

Simm was beginning to understand why there had been several attempts made on the figurehead's life.

Though, of course, the main way the DG acceded to the position was through a series of strategic assassinations, so it was only fair that other ambitious officers did the same.

But the politics of the situation were getting out of hand, and he realised that the time was coming when he would have to take a side - the Directorate, or its current leader.

Or more realistically, the current DG, and however many challengers there were.

And the only person he could talk to about his concerns was in a care facility undertaking intensive physical therapy.

The medics had barely removed her from his office when all the little niggles had started rising to the surface.

Smythe had arrived unannounced, and the first thing he'd done was throw her personal possessions in the bin.

Not reported for duty.

Not handed over his orders.

Not even acknowledged his new boss.

Simm had gone out to ask one of her colleagues to step in, and found the boy making himself at home at her desk when he got back.

The boy's barely concealed contempt for his new boss made him wonder what the Smythes senior had said about him.

Not that it mattered.

Simm was determined to get rid of him, and get Evans back as soon as possible.

It was her plant decorating his bookshelf, and after some sharp words to the boy, he'd taken the rest of her things and kept them in an archive box in his office.

Perhaps he was too sharp, and perhaps if the boy had followed protocol and reported in first, they might have got off to a better start.

But Simm's gut feel was the boy was a spy reporting back to someone else, who was intent on replacing him as Director of the Propaganda Bureau.

That he was about to find himself with a different, less important job, in a different department in a district far, far away.

Or perhaps a casualty of someone else's tilt for the leadership.

Maybe he needed to get out to that care facility and see what Evans knew.

Preferably before the boy ballsed up anything important.

Stuck in rehab or not, she always had her finger on the pulse, and today felt like a good day for a sitrep.

He stood and paced up and down his office, ostensibly thinking deeply, but really waiting for the boy to absent himself for long enough to permit a clean getaway.

He wondered whether to lock up his files, but reasoned that one way or another, the boy already knew the gist of most of it. And he probably couldn't cock anything else up any further than he already had.

Though it was uncertain whether Simm could recover his reputation.

After a point, the boy left, and Simm sloped out of the office and into the stairwell. Ran down several flights, crossed to the other side of the building and caught a lift to the basement carpool.

At the counter, he signed the appropriate requisitions for a car and driver and was soon in a black executive vehicle on his way.

The driver cleared his throat, and when Simm looked at him, he asked, "You're January Evans' commanding officer?"

Simm nodded.

"Is she doing well?"

"So far, so good."

"If you don't mind me asking Sir, do you know anything of the circumstances of the incident?"

"She slipped on the resurfaced floor."

The driver frowned, "may I speak freely Sir?"

Simm narrowed his eyes slightly, assessing the driver, then nodded his assent.

"There are rumours in the lower ranks it wasn't an accident, and she wasn't the intended target."

The driver glanced at him in the rear-view mirror before looking back at the road.

Simm considered the news.

Not out of line with what he'd been thinking, but the attack, if it was an attack on him, came sooner than expected.

"Do the rumours have any other information to add?"

"You might want to keep an eye on Smythe."

That goddamned boy.

Simm frowned, also in keeping with his thoughts.

"Thank you driver."

Not much later, they passed through the gates of the rehabilitation hospital.

The driver got out of the car, opened the door, and saluted as Simm climbed out. "Would you like me to wait Sir?"

Simm smiled slightly, "if you're prepared to be my alibi, you may wait in the mess hall Private..."

"Langley Sir."

"I'll call for you when I'm ready to leave Langley."

"Uh, Sir?"

"Yes Private."

"Please pass my best wishes on to Captain Evans Sir."

Simm nodded and returned the salute before turning and jogging up the stairs and through the hospital doors.

Her room was empty, and an attendant directed him to the loggia.

The loggia was an outdoor area within the ground floor footprint of the main building, like a room that was missing three walls.

Patients with various levels of ability and assistance were walking up and down.

Others, like Evans, were sitting, or lying, around the edges, looking out over a garden and across the City in the distance.

More sat at tables on the lawn or walking along paths between the garden beds.

Evans saw him coming and rose to salute.

He saluted in return and gestured for her to sit.

She shook her head slightly, picked up a cane, and took a few steps out to the lawn.

He rushed to catch up and take her arm.

Evans stiffened for a moment but allowed herself to relax and lean into him, gesturing to a table with her cane.

He nodded, "how is the rehab coming along?"

"I'm tired and sore, but the doctor says I'm fit for light duties."

"That's great news, but do you have any idea what they think light duties are?"

She laughed, "not yet, though I expect it'll all be lister out on the Return to Service orders."

"Then I shall have to see what they recommend and work out how I can make it easy for you."

He pulled a chair out for her, and she sat, "thank you Sir, I appreciate that."

He dragged another chair closer, and arranged it so they were facing each other, and between them, had an excellent view of all approaches.

He scanned the surroundings, "I heard that your accident may not have been an accident and that you may not have been the target."

She looked passed him as she replied, "yes, I've heard that too. Who told you?"

"Private Langley. He seems a little sweet on you."

"Langley, Langley, Langley... Motor pool Langley?"

"Yes, that's the one."

"Ah. He's a credible source. Did he say anything else?"

"When he dropped me off, he asked me to pass his best wishes on to you."

"Is he waiting for you?"

Simm nodded.

"Right. Do you think you could send for him so I can speak with him while you query my Return to Service orders?"

"Naaaww. Are you sweet on him too?"

"Oh, for god's sake, did you not just hear me say he was a credible source? The comms lines are monitored, so we need to speak face to face where they can't overhear us."

Simm cleared his throat, "oh. I see. Uh, I expect you'd like me to do that now?"

"If it's not too much trouble Sir."

"How much time do you need?"

"At least 15 minutes."

Simm looked at his watch, "shouldn't be too hard."

He walked back to the loggia and asked one of the attending therapists to send for his driver and page the doctor.

And before too long, he was in an untidy office discussing Evans' return conditions.

She was doing well, and they could discharge her today as long as there was someone to help her out at home.

And no, barracks didn't count.

She needed to maximise her movement and limit her sitting; starting at half an hour at a time and working up.

She'd need a cane for a few months. It would limit her ability to carry things.

She'd be on pain medication and would need to continue her rehabilitation for perhaps as long as six months.

She'd be tired until she built up some stamina and endurance. She should start her return with half-days, working up to full days over the next few weeks.

But she must be careful not to overdo it, or she'd find herself back in residential rehab.

It was all manageable within the scope of her duties. Even at half-time, she was more efficient than the boy, though according to Langley, there was more going on there than met the eye.

With Return to Service orders, her potentially useful superpower, and his right to choose his assistant, his prospects for getting her back were better than ordinary.

Simm didn't see any obstacles, but it remained to be seen what Langley might bring to their attention.

With a spring in his step, he returned to Evans.

Langley stood, saluted, then turned and walked a few paces away. He was still within earshot, but back to them, looked as though he was admiring the view of the City.

"All good," Simm said, "if there's someone to care for you at home, you can leave today and return to your duties tomorrow."

Evans stood and gave her hip a soothing rub.

"Right, that's good news. It seems we don't have much time."

"Much time?"

"I can't tell you more than that. Their plans are in progress, and we can't have you giving the game away."

"The game?"

"Yes John."

And Simm wondered for a moment if he'd already picked a side.

And whether it was the right one.

But Evans was an excellent assistant - and she'd said and done nothing to make him suspect her. There were no obvious reasons to distrust her now.

"Are you going to be all right?"

"Yes. You just need to act normal for a week or so while we," she gestured at Langley's back, "get this sorted out."

"Are you going to be all right?"

She laughed, "of course Sir. All those associations and cliques and so on are not what they seem."

"You're not really an assistant are you Evans?"

"No Sir, I'm not. But I can't tell you what I am."

"Of course not.

"But after this incident?"

"Well, let's wait and see."

Langley helped him get her packed and into the car. They dropped her back at her apartment. The one Simm knew she lived alone in.

She assured him she'd be fine. She'd be taken care of.

The drive back to the office was a quiet one. There was so much he wanted to know, but he didn't know where to start.

Assuming he had the clearance to know.

And in any case, he doubted Langley would give him answers.

How could Evans not be an assistant? She'd worked for him for years, and he'd had no idea she was anything more than an exceptionally bright young woman.

Had she qualified at University and gone deep undercover?

Was she even injured?

He struggled to get through the week.

He expected goons with guns to break in at any moment. Or some kind of enormous announcement on the news feed.

But there was nothing.

If anything, each day was more ordinary than the last.

The meetings were even more tedious, the boy even more incompetent, even more paperwork piling up in his tray.

At every turn, he hit a blank, featureless wall of ordinariness.

By the time Monday came around again, he was at peak restlessness, so when he saw Evans at her desk, he was unusually effusive in his greeting.

She followed him into his office, leaning on a cane with one hand, carrying a notebook in the other.

He opened his mouth to question her, but she cut him off.

"I can't tell you anything," she said, "you don't have the clearance."

"I beg your pardon? What do you mean I don't have clearance?"

"It's an operational matter Sir."

He grunted, "operational matter."

"Yes Sir, outside your purview."

"But if it was about me, surely I deserve to know."

"I can't possibly comment."

He sat behind his desk and waved at the chairs in front of it.

Smiling, she sat down and leaned her cane against the desk.

"And what about you Evans?"

"Clean bill of health Sir,"

"That's not what I meant, and you know it."

"Well, I'd like my plant back Sir."

"You're staying?"

"Yes Sir. I'm staying."

"Oh, thank goodness."

He didn't know what her job really was, but she was an excellent assistant, and he was glad to have her back.

THE END

36

ALEXANDRIA BLAELOCK

AUTHOR OF FATE IN YOUR HANDS

CALLING IT A DAY

A SECURITY DIRECTORATE SHORT STORY

CALLING IT A DAY

The phone box was red.

She wanted to call it pillar box red, but did not know where the words came from.

Or what they meant - what was a pillar box?

The box had a domed top with four walls made of small glass panes. Six tall, three wide, set into wood beading, all painted red, and joined at the corners with lines of vertically striped moulding.

Like a stick of rock candy, though she did not know what those words meant or where they came from either.

The box didn't have a phone inside it, but above the door was a sign that said telephone, surmounted by a moulded crown.

She had an urge to curl her blue gloved fingers under the elegant domed handle and pull the door open.

The box made her feel light and bouncy.

As if there should be laughing.

And skipping.

And the taste of sweetness in her mouth.

Her hair in bouncy puppy dog tails hanging over her ears.

The feeling was as unusual as it was unexpected and set her nerves on fire.

She didn't know where it came from, or why it was so different from the darkness she usually felt.

It was disturbing.

And uncomfortable.

It made her regulation chignon feel too tight, and the weight of her uniform cap too heavy.

Captain Maeryn Prothero turned her back on the perplexing box and looked out over the junk yard her unit was currently searching.

That was more like it. The cold application of logic to the problem at hand, and fortunately, her career had progressed far enough that it was no longer her hands combing the site for evidence.

Her job was to direct the search, analyse the results, and arrest the guilty.

She shoved her hands in the pockets of her navy-blue greatcoat so she wasn't tempted to mess with her hair, annoyed she felt the need.

Both to mess her hair *and* to restrain herself.

A Eugenics Programme success, she'd passed the Genomics Bureau post-natal testing, survived the State Academy of Cultural Regulation with a useful genetic "superpower" and graduated from the University of Civilisation with an advantageous qualification.

All so long ago, she barely remembered it.

It was a very long time since she'd taken her first posting at the Bureau of Internal Investigations, yet here she was, losing her cool like a newbie to an inanimate object.

In a swirl of greatcoat tails, she stalked a few paces away so the box couldn't see her, and instantly felt better.

She barked a few orders at the goons and felt better still.

That was more like her, not to mention she had a hard-arse reputation to maintain.

Actually, being a hard-arse was her "superpower," a genetic gift courtesy of the Security Directorate Eugenics Program.

Always assuming you thought extreme impassivity was a gift, but it made her good at hunting out and executing traitors.

A gift that almost, but not quite, made up for her unusually angular, darkly hirsute ugliness. Not to mention the ridiculously witchy wart on her nose she hadn't got around to removing yet.

She'd never failed to solve a case, and she'd never failed a mission.

Incredibly, she found her thoughts returning to the box.

Was it possible someone had the kind of "superpower" that might allow them to add something to an inanimate object to repel the curious? Would it work on the marginally gifted and normals as well?

Should someone actually have such a power, to use it without the proper authorisation was treasonous.

She'd have it sent back to the lab and get it checked out.

A small, delicate woman approached and waited for acknowledgement.

"Simms," Prothero nodded.

"Ma'am," she saluted, and Prothero sketched a reply.

"We've searched the offices and car yard, and nothing so far."

Prothero grunted. Simms' shoulders started turning away, but immediately swivelled back when her boss cleared her throat.

"There's something bothering me about the phone box," she said, pointing a thumb over her shoulder, "have it sent back to the lab with whatever else you find."

"Yes Ma'am."

"I'll head back now. Let me know when you get in."

"Ma'am."

Prothero turned and walked away, back to the car, catching her driver by surprise. She didn't bother reprimanding him, just climbed in, leaving him scrambling to catch up.

«« • »»

The wait for information about the phone box was tedious.

She immersed herself in reviewing the progress of ongoing investigations.

She visited the warehouses to inspect the relevant evidences, but they were an excuse to visit the box. To prowl around it, hands clasped behind her back, fascinated yet repelled by it.

42

Technicians had analysed the manufacturing materials.

Sensitives had examined it for evidence of superpower application.

There was absolutely nothing to suggest there was anything out of the ordinary about it.

It was exactly what it appeared to be.

And yet she couldn't let it go.

«« • »»

When the psych evaluation reminder popped up on her screen, she was ludicrously relieved and immediately left her desk.

In general, she believed the mandatory quarterly evaluations were critical for the ongoing efficiency of everyone at a lower rank than captain.

In her line of work, investigators were regularly exposed to the worst of the worst, and it was essential to ensure none of her operatives were suborned in any way.

But at her level, with her security clearance, they were a waste of time.

Normally she'd reschedule them until they threatened her with disciplinary action before attending.

But this time, the idea of hoops to jump through was a welcome distraction.

In the blindingly white clinical rooms, Dr Kov's receptionist was so surprised to see her she couldn't string together a coherent sentence.

Prothero ignored her, ignoring the white plastic chairs and cheery motivational posters, pacing up and down the waiting area until she was called into his retro wood panelled rooms.

Still restless, she shoved her hands into her pockets and threw herself onto the patient couch. A surprisingly comfortable kind of scuffed tan leather sling supported by a curved chrome cradle resting on a blackened metal stand.

"So Prothero," he said, swivelling his chair away from his no nonsense wooden desk to look at her, "what's on your mind?"

"What makes you think there's something on my mind?"

"You're here aren't you? You haven't tried to re-schedule even once."

She slumped lower into the couch, "ah."

"Shall we do the usual dance Captain, or seeing as you're here more or less willingly, shall we get straight to the nub of the matter?"

Prothero closed her eyes and screwed her face up, like a child forced to eat green vegetables.

"Yes, I can suspend you, but my job is to take care of you, so you can take care of the Directorate. Rest assured, I won't be doing that unless I think you're a danger to yourself and others."

"Fine." She sighed, "we were searching a junk yard for evidence, and we found a phone box. And the idea of it makes me uncomfortable."

"I see, and why do you think that is."

"I don't know. There's nothing to suggest it is in any way unusual, but I can't stop thinking about it."

"How mysterious. Do you have a theory?"

"I'm not sure. I wondered if it was significant in some way, but I don't recall seeing anything like it before."

"The Directorate is experimenting with a hypnosis treatment modality. Would you like me to seek authorisation to add you to the program?"

"Hypnosis? What does that involve?"

"Well, used as a treatment for trauma, it helps to dissociate the trauma and remodel the experiences more positively."

"And what makes you think it might help me and the phone box?"

"It might be possible to recover experiences you've forgotten or blocked out, and reintegrate them into your psyche."

"Reintegrate what now?"

"Just think of it as resolving your issues."

"Okay. But will it work?"

"There's a good chance it will make things better, but there's a slight chance it'll make your situation worse."

"Aahhh. Okay.

"Let's do it then."

Kov cleared his throat, "right. Well. Given the secure nature of the work you undertake, I need to get permission to try it on you. You may get permission to receive the treatment, but I may be required to pass you onto a different therapist."

"I'm not sure I'm comfortable with that."

"Well, let's seek permission and see what comes back."

Prothero growled.

"How long will that take?"

"Shouldn't be more than a day or two, I wouldn't think."

"Fine fine fine. Let's do that."

"I'll call you when I know more."

«« • »»

In fact, it was almost a week before Prothero heard anything further.

The week included a series of gruelling court-martial testimonies, followed by a death sentence, and performing the resulting execution.

So when the notice of the appointment with Kov came, she was pleased to see it.

Without question, she took the offered sedative and made herself comfortable on the sling couch.

She followed Kov's prompts, and before long found herself in a different universe.

Running along a beach.

The sun was setting on her left in a blaze of orange and purple; the vibrancy of the sky was turning the clear blue water into shades of grey, and the yellow sand a darker grey.

To her right, grasses grew in clumps, but she was trying not to look because someone was chasing her.

Her head was down as she pumped her tiny arms and legs.

They were on fire with pain, and she wasn't sure how much longer she could keep running.

Her breath was getting stuck in her lungs as she tried to gasp it out and breathe in fresh.

It didn't matter.

She had to keep running because if she stopped, something bad would happen.

Someone grabbed her shoulder, and she screamed, high and sharp and shrill.

Dr Kov said something, and her mind went blank.

He said something else, and she saw a red phone box.

It was very tall, or perhaps she was very small.

The sun was high in the sky, and she was sitting on a bench on the other side of the road, swinging her legs backwards and forwards as she watched the people walk by.

Her father nudged her with his elbow, and she giggled and tossed her head, making the twin hair tails hanging over her ears swing in the light breeze from the ocean.

She licked chocolate ice cream from the top of her cone, then licked the melting ice cream from her hand and the bottom of the cone, racing to eat it all before the cone dissolved.

He nudged her again, and she jumped off the bench, taking his hand as they walked across the road, onto the pier.

He played some kind of shooting game, and she cheered and clapped and dropped her ice cream and started crying.

He won her a small white teddy bear, then bought her a stick of hard peppermint flavoured rock. Red on the outside, and white on the inside, with some words she couldn't read on the inside. He unwrapped one end for her and stole a lick or two for quality control before he gave it to her to try.

It was so sweet it made her tongue curl.

She loved it.

Joy flooded her tiny body as thoroughly as the sugar from the rock.

They followed the sound of tinny music to a carousel at the end of the pier. He put her on a snow-white horse with a gold mane and turquoise livery and waved at her as she passed him.

She laughed and waved back and swore to herself she would remember this day forever.

And then she came around again, and Daddy was nowhere to be seen.

"Daddy?" she called, but there was no answer.

She stood as high as the stirrups would allow, scanning the crowd as the carousel made another circuit before slowing and stopping.

"Daddy?" she cried a little louder, running for the exit, turning around and around looking for him.

And then she saw him, dragged away by big men wearing black.

So she ran down the pier as fast as her legs could carry her, screaming "Daddy" as she chased them off the end and along the street.

Still running, still screaming, as she watched the men bundle him into a black van.

Still screaming as one of them turned and started running towards her.

She closed her mouth, wheeled silently and ran away, across the road, and down along the sand.

Kov said something, and her mind went blank.

He said some other things, and her breathing and heart rate slowed.

He said some more, and she drifted into a gentle sleep.

«« • »»

When she woke, she was back in her tiny one-room flat. The one allocated for her first posting and she'd never got round to applying for something else.

With just enough room for a bed and a chair. On one wall, next to a glass doored Juliet balcony overlooking the seafront, a cupboard housing a sink and a one burner electric stove. And on the other, next to the blue entry door, one shelf with a hanging rack.

A little disoriented, not knowing how she got there.

But calm.

She remembered seeing Dr Kov, taking a pill, and going to sleep.

Then nothing.

She assumed she'd passed her psych evaluation and was grateful to have got out of that bureaucratic nightmare unscathed.

She poured herself a glass of wine, opened the door, and leaned on the Juliet balcony railing as she looked down and out, over the sparkling water, taking deep breaths of the fresh sea air.

After a moment, she realised she was hungry, but chose to lean her elbows on the balcony and enjoy the view a little longer.

It had been a long week.

There was plenty of time for a stroll along the seafront, and for sharing some fish and chips with the seagulls.

As she turned back to the room, a grey, threadbare stuffed toy caught her eye. She frowned at it, trying to remember where it came from, or why she had it.

She shook her head as she picked it up and dropped it in the bin on her way out the door.

Life was hard enough without filling her house up with old rubbish.

THE END

ALEXANDRIA
BLAELOCK
AUTHOR OF FATE IN YOUR HANDS
VENI VIDI VICI
A SECURITY DIRECTORATE SHORT STORY

VENI VIDI VICI

Cora was a Eugenics Programme success.

She'd passed the Genomics Bureau post-natal testing, survived the State Academy of Cultural Regulation with a useful genetic "super-power" and graduated from the University of Civilisation with an advantageous qualification.

So spending the next few weeks manually weeding the vegetable bed, pruning the fruit trees, and keeping the lush growth of whatever the prickly native vegetation was under control was bad enough without alarms going off to boot.

She'd more or less just arrived at Exploratorem Station, and despite all the drills, hadn't heard that particular sequence of tones, and didn't know what it meant.

Alert or alarmed?

Evacuate quickly or assemble nearby and return slowly?

Grab a gun and prepare for invasion?

It was vexing.

Had she just gone through the most useless induction on the planet?

Security clearances notwithstanding, surely the most basic of site education programmes should include identification and explanation of all alarm codes.

She frowned and inspected her chafed and blister scarred hands as she stood, stretching out her aching back and arms while looking around to see what the others were doing.

There was not a human to be seen, only the open fields of red dirt bisected by waist height fences made of dried offcuts of the cut back native vegetation. Towards the distance, a small, faded green corrugated tin tool shed with a gable roof at the entrance to the productive gardens, and further off in the distance, the station itself.

Criminal to leave her out here on her own.

The point of newbies and returnees working in the fields was not just food production. It was acclimatising as quickly as possible to the altitude, the climate, and the air-borne spores that were toxic to some.

Which meant someone should be here supervising her.

If she could not adjust, the local command needed to isolate and treat her before sending her back to the City on the next convoy out for redeployment.

Assuming she was fit to take up another post and avoid an untimely transfer to the Euthanasia Programme.

This lack of supervision was negligent.

Then again, she was a recent graduate - a very new, very junior officer, so perhaps this was just code for some stupid hazing ritual. Leave her alone and set off some kind of alarm.

Watch, laughing, from the control room to see what she did.

She frowned for a moment, then looked more attentively around her.

The air was clear; no sign of environmental or surface disturbances.

Birds sang in the fencing and trees, so nothing unusual enough to send them squawking away in alarm.

The light breeze drying her sweaty brow smelled pleasantly floral. No hint of smoke or chemical contaminants.

Except for the scentless, tasteless, invisible spores she was here to interact with, there didn't appear to be any danger.

No reason to return to base, no reason to evacuate, no reason to take action at all.

So, if this was a hazing ritual, there'd probably be some kind of embarrassing prank set up for her when she returned to base. Some sort of physical trial that would set off alarms, spray her with something unpleasant or staining, or just plain running the gauntlet while her new colleagues attempted to land a punch, kick, or noxious projectile.

Maybe some other painful and humiliating scenario that would dog her for the rest of her career.

Irritating.

She curled her lip.

Best keep working until the lunch break, then stun them with her equanimity when she returned to base. If the alarm was something urgent or important, no doubt an officer would send for her.

Annoyed as well as stubborn, she bent once more to her weeding. At this point, she didn't have a security clearance, so diligent work on her assigned task would probably earn more credit than standing around gawping and getting in the way.

Regardless of the state of her hands, back and legs.

Not forgetting her brain, which seemed to be stagnating.

But given the usual environmental conditions weren't the best for growing, you had to get out and work the fields while you could.

Unsocial at the best of times, she'd found Exploratorem's spartan life suited her.

A minimal crew, living a monastic lifestyle. Limited communication with the outside world, though Cora didn't yet know whether that was something to do with the location or some kind of security embargo she hadn't been told about yet.

Everyone on the crew, except maybe the station director, rotated through several standard shifts over the days, weeks and months. Aside from their regular assigned duties, there was hard physical labour in the fields growing the food.

Then time spent cooking and preserving the food and brewing beer, maintenance of equipment and machinery, plus the random security and evacuation drills.

Which made it all the more curious; why didn't she know what this alarm meant.

Was it another security clearance blockage?

While it felt insulting, there wasn't much point learning more about what the station did until they all knew she'd be completing her assignment rather than heading back to the City.

When her posting was announced, a murmur had run through the University auditorium.

Everyone had heard of Exploratorem, and the harsh life endured there, but no one knew precisely what function Exploratorem performed.

Wild rumours about activities like covert surveillance, interrogations and mind control were everywhere, but given you weren't supposed to talk about your work, that was probably just trash talk filling the vacuum of fact.

She couldn't help feeling a little smug that she was the one who was going to find out.

Cora's "superpower" was influence. She couldn't control minds *per se*, but she could encourage them to *lean* in a particular direction. It didn't surprise her that the future would involve her power - it was what she'd trained for, after all.

And having just scraped past her physical final, Cora knew she wasn't going to the station for anything other than her brilliant mind.

Most people took one look at her petite busty body, and that was that. She owned them, no need to consider the application of her superpower.

Her unusually bright green eyes snared those who looked higher, some even noticing their setting in a cute, heart-shaped face surrounded by long, wavy blonde hair.

However, those who assumed she was a pushover were generally surprised to find otherwise, but not for long.

Her outer beauty disguised an icy heart, ruthless spirit and steel spine. She was a triumph of social conditioning.

She'd worked hard to build up her dumb blonde persona with revealing clothes and a breathy voice. It allowed her to more easily manipulate her opponents and gave her the element of surprise when leveraged with her quick reflexes.

Though the amount of physical labour she'd endured in the fields and kitchens during the last couple of weeks had not only improved the quality of her sleep, but her muscle strength and tone too.

Plus, she'd gained a light tan that made her look as healthy as she felt, though she could've done without the freckles that now sprinkled her nose.

But they added to her armoury; in the right circumstances, they'd be disarming.

Shame she hadn't been this fit for the physical final, though if she'd done better, who knew where she'd be now?

And she had the feeling that Exploratorem was going to be right up her alley.

Cora lugged her trug of weeds to the compost heap and emptied it.

Was life at the station austere to keep the mind sharp, or was it an intensive boot camp style muscle building training camp preparing junior officers for some other placement?

Given her power, an assassin perhaps?

The siren for lunch finally sounded.

Cora collected her tools together, cleaned and stowed them in the tool shed before dusting her hands off on the legs of her boiler suit and walking towards the station.

As she got closer, she felt her heart rate increase in anticipation of the hazing prank and started looking more carefully for triggers. But it all seemed perfectly normal until she reached the squat, concrete sentry box.

The marine inside did not challenge her as he had done every other time she'd returned from the fields. In fact, he didn't acknowledge her in any way. Just sat at silent attention, staring out the window, not meeting her gaze.

Not moving a muscle.

She rapped on the window, but he didn't flinch or even look at her.

Her annoyance was increasing; given everything else, she was at threat level three at this point.

He was just a goon, after all. At the very least, he should acknowledge her as his superior with a nod or a "ma'am".

She could understand why the more senior officers might choose to haze her, but goons as well? This was beyond a joke.

She stalked around the box and ripped the door open.

He fell backwards out of the box, tumbling off his seat onto the ground.

Cora jumped back on guard, expecting him to rise and attempt to subdue her, but he lay where he fell.

She stretched her leg out and poked him with a safety booted toe, but he remained unresponsive.

Somewhat reassured, she crouched and checked his pulse.

It took her several attempts to realise he didn't have a pulse.

Curious.

But annoyingly extreme for a prank.

When she took the news back to the station, what would they want to know?

Cora examined the body. Its uniform and boots were clean, crisp, and intact. There were no visible signs of trauma, smelling of standard-issue soap. There didn't seem to be anything to indicate a cause of death.

She moved onto the sentry box. No visible damage internally or externally. No sign of a spill, electrical malfunction, or tampering. Aside from her boot prints, there was no disturbance to the ground.

All in all, nothing to suggest causality.

She reached into the box and picked up the radio handset, clicking the call button a couple of times to attract attention from the station.

There was no response.

She didn't yet know Exploratorem's security protocols, but more widely, radio communications required the receiver to acknowledge transmission and engage scrambling before communication could commence.

She clicked the call button another couple of times.

Still no response.

She ground her teeth.

Idiots, all of them.

Was this still a prank, or, given the dead soldier something more serious?

She put the radio handset back in its place and, leaving the body where it was, headed into the prickly native vegetation alongside the road for a more circumspect approach to the main station building.

As she prowled through the bush, she was alert to changes in the environment, but the conditions remained as innocuous as when the alarm first sounded.

Aside from the dead marine and unresponsive radio, there was nothing to suggest that this day was any different from any other she'd spent here.

Perhaps something like this scenario had been the basis of her final physical exam. She'd learnt a lot from her debriefing, but hadn't expected to be an unarmed one-woman assault party on her own station.

At least not anytime soon anyway.

With only a few metres to go, she slowed her pace still further and examined the station façade.

The walls were smooth and unbroken, the gravel of the road and car park were no more choppy than usual. Three station all-terrain vehicles parked in an orderly row down one side of the parking area.

Doors were all neatly closed with no evidence of attack, abrupt arrival or departure.

All as expected, with no signs of an external assault.

That didn't rule out a quick, clean, surgical assault with enemy agents waiting inside the station, but it made that scenario less likely.

From her limited political knowledge, the only viable enemy was rebels, and they were scum who didn't have the organisation, aptitude or technical skills for a precision strike.

Which, assuming the goon did not die of natural causes, left either an armed internal assault or some kind of silent chemical or electrical attack.

Was there such a thing that could simultaneously disable both the station and a moron in a box a few hundred metres away?

An electromagnetic pulse could disable the equipment, but was there something similar that could disable people too?

Human brains were mostly electric, so theoretically, it was possible to do both. She hadn't heard of this kind of weapon as an actual device, or in development, but you'd need a security clearance of the highest level to know for sure.

If such a device had been deployed at Exploratorem, would it have fired once or still be "on?"

Though if it were on, she wouldn't have made it this far, so she probably didn't need to worry about her brain frying from the inside out.

In any case, she couldn't stand around out there all day. She had to get inside the station before she could determine her next steps.

It was possible she'd avoided detection to this point, but thanks to not having a security clearance, she'd no choice but to enter via the front door. If whoever it was didn't know she was here now, they soon would.

And if they knew she was there, they'd be expecting her to arrive for lunch anyway.

Hopefully, this was the most meticulously planned and implemented hazing prank ever known in the Security Directorate.

But just in case, she set her hair loose and fluffed it up before pulling the zipper of her boiler suit down a little lower to expose the lace edges of her bra. Deciding that wasn't enough, she rolled her sleeves and pants up to reveal a little more skin.

She pulled a small branch of leaves from a nearby tree, then popped back onto the road and starting walking leisurely towards the station, swinging her hips and fanning herself with the branch.

Looking like a sexy, and clueless woman on a day trip to the country.

Her influence was the most effective at close quarters, and completely ineffective when viewed on a screen at a distance. Even so, she generated an influence of "poor, lazy little rich girl, completely out of her depth."

It might not help with those in the station, but it reminded her she had a persona to work with.

Her skinned crawled, and her heart was beating like crazy, but there wasn't really an alternative to walking in the open.

The closer she got to the station, the harder it was to force her body to keep moving forward.

Bit of a shame she couldn't influence herself as easily as others.

Arriving at the front door without challenge, when she held her security card over the reader, it surprised her to find it already open.

It was possible the entry security system was separate from the primary system, but not likely.

So if the security was working, the entire station should be too.

She pushed open the door to find the entryway empty. She took a long step sideways into a corner and stood still and silent to listen.

Aside from the buzz of the single light flickering, all was quiet.

At this time of day, she should've been able to hear the murmur of conversation. There should be computers pinging when they picked up whatever they were looking for. There should be phones and printers and drawers slamming.

But aside from her beating heart, all was quiet.

Cora felt as though her skin had crawled right off her body, leaving all her nerves exposed.

Whatever was going on felt very, very wrong.

And given that, she'd feel a whole lot better with a gun in her hand.

Next stop, the armoury, which fortunately was just around the corner.

She sidled along the corridor, back to the wall, generating an "I'm not here" influence. She didn't see anyone, living or dead, as she inched around the corner towards the armoury.

Risking exposure, she ducked her head through the doorway and saw an armourer slumped over the counter, but nothing else was obviously suspicious.

She stepped into the room, tensed on her toes, ready to leap back. The armourer remained static; no projectiles fired in her direction.

Nothing happened.

Looking as closely as she could at the room, given the flickering light from the hall, she found nothing that seemed unusual.

Or more unusual than this already unusual situation, at any rate.

She took the armourer's pulse, and he too did not have one.

Station policy required guns be sealed in the cage behind the armourer's counter, and she would (of course) not have access. Taking a step back, she vaulted across the desk and slid to the ground behind it, dislodging the armourer in the process.

He fell to the floor with a crash, and she dived for cover under a bar set up for cleaning the guns.

She forced herself to be still, and blood pounding in her ears, she took a deep breath and held it while she slowly counted.

One.

Two.

Three.

Four.

Five.
Six.
Seven.
Eight.
Nine.
Ten.
No alarms, no movement.

She let her breath out in a big sigh, enjoying the momentary feeling of relief as her shoulders dropped and the built-up tension in her body released.

Then she pulled herself to her feet, grabbed a rifle from a rack and rummaged around looking for preloaded magazines. One for the rifle, locked and loaded, plus a bunch in the pockets of her suit.

While she didn't really think this was a prank any longer, if it was, she didn't want her colleagues thinking she wasn't willing to do what had to be done to save them.

And in fact, by this point, she was so annoyed she really hoped there was someone out there to viciously shoot up.

As she opened the door of the armoury cage, she noticed the armourer's body again.

The station was climate controlled, and she had no idea whether the air was canned or mixed with fresh air from outside.

What if it had been a chemical attack or spill and there was some poisonous residue still circulating in the station's air?

Worst-case scenario, something like poison tainted the air, and she would die before she could alert the Director General's Office.

How pathetic.

Best-case scenario, she shouldered a re-breather and saved the day.

She grabbed a re-breather and pulled it on as she walked towards the corridor, psyching herself up to step back into it.

She briefly considered calling out to the station crew for assistance, but the gut instincts that ensured she survived the Academy of Cultural Regulation were telling her not to draw attention to herself.

The next target should probably be the control centre, to see if it was operational and whether there was any data about the incident.

Or, given that there was a limit to what one short junior officer without a security clearance could do, external communication back to the City.

As you'd expect, it was a secure panic room style office in the centre of the building. And she didn't know the exact path to find it.

Or whether she'd be able to gain entry.

Thanks for nothing Security Chief.

But if this was a "situation," and if they needed help, she had to get to the control room.

Radiating her "I'm not here" influence, Cora sidled out of the room and back into the corridor.

At first, the corridors were clear, but as she neared the mess hall, rifle at the ready, she started seeing the bodies of her colleagues. Sprawled haphazardly, as if a puppet master had just cut their strings.

She stopped to examine the first few to find that, like the marine and armourer, they had no pulse and no obvious cause of death.

Losers, all of them.

With no external air getting through the rebreather, Cora couldn't tell whether there was food cooking or burning, so she checked the kitchen to see if there was any sign of what time the incident, whatever it was, had occurred.

Even more bodies were piled up in the mess, but she didn't bother to give them more than a cursory glance to see if any were moving.

Similarly, the kitchen contained several bodies. One had collapsed over the grill was charring gently, so she pulled him off it in case he set the place on fire.

Forgetting she wasn't wearing a watch; she checked her wrist against the kitchen clock and made a note to never take it off again.

She checked a random body to find its watch matched the clock. Going by how hungry she was, she deduced the clock had the right time.

Food was prepped and ready to cook, but cooking hadn't begun. Which suggested the incident had occurred sometime between mid-morning and the first lunch service. Maybe an hour or two ago.

And given people had died on their way into the mess, it probably wasn't something in the food.

Cora turned to leave the kitchen through the other door and noticed a rat by the wall. Giving it a poke with the rifle barrel, she wasn't really surprised that it didn't move. Though the rigidity of its body compared to those of the crew was surprising.

She remembered reading somewhere that rodents go outside to die. So was it possible that contamination in the air system had slowly built to a dose lethal to humans?

Though if that was the case, how had the marine died in the sentry box a few hundred metres away?

A slow-acting poison?

Cora massaged her temples before snuggling the rifle back into her shoulder and heading out.

The still emptiness of the usually noisy, bustling station was unsettling. Not to mention the piles of inexplicably dead people.

She was finding it more difficult to control her emotions and feeling her self-control slipping.

A while later, after walking up and down a few more corridors, she came across the control room door.

At least, the red-lit room full of brightly lit screens and panels of flashing lights seen through the window of the double blast doors looked like it might be a control room.

It could have been a decoy room, but the bodies slumped over the computer terminals suggested the room had a legitimate purpose.

Not that it mattered. She had to get in.

But first, a quick reconnoitre up and back the corridor looking for concealed enemy agents. Not that there was much in the way of hiding places, aside from more unmarked corpses.

Trying not to shudder, she focused on the access panel next to the door.

It was a large panel with access modes including card reader, PIN keypad, hand reader, and retinal scanner.

And a steadily glowing red light.

There was no way she was going to be able to break the door down, so the only option was to try the access controls one by one and see what happened.

Tucking the rifle under her armpit, and crossing her fingers, she swiped her card. The light flashed green for a moment along with what seemed, in the silence, a deafening beep.

She pulled the door, but nothing happened.

Next, she tried the PIN she used to access her sleeping quarters, and again the light flashed green with a beep.

But still the door didn't open.

"Fuck."

She let out a sigh and looked up at the ceiling.

She rubbed her sweaty right hand down the leg of her pants and placed it on the reader.

It was cool to the touch, but started heating up rapidly.

She knew this was a tool to warn off unauthorised personnel, and also knew that if she wasn't authorised, the pad would continue to heat until she removed her hand or it burned her skin off.

She was just about at the point where the pain was too great to continue when the light flashed and the device beeped.

Cora snatched her hand back and pressed it to her breast until the pain lessened.

She pulled the door, and it still didn't open.

"Fuck's sake!"

She stamped a little dance and kicked the door violently several times.

Then groaned and laid her forehead against the door. There was no choice now but to try the retina scanner.

If they hadn't transferred her retinal print to the station, or hadn't authorised it, the scanner would blind her.

And more or less useless for the current incident and perhaps the rest of her career.

But there was no other way.

She had to try.

Not that they gave you medals for trying.

She took a deep breath, squeezed her eyes shut, and counted to ten.

Then, before she could change her mind, she put her face in front of the scanner and tried not to flinch as the laser flashed for what seemed like eternity and her vision failed her.

She closed her eyes, trying not to sob, trying not to think about a one-dimensional future with an eye patch.

Then she heard a beep and a clunk as the door unlocked.

A single tear escaped her eye and slid down her cheek.

She opened her eyes; and found she could see. Just momentarily dazzled by the brightness of the laser.

But there was no time for hysterics. She had a job to do.

Despite her success at gaining entry to the control room, she was a little embarrassed to find she could probably have gained entrance more or less any time she wanted. It was a testament to the strength of her training that she hadn't tried.

Or had someone inside set it up as they were dying?

Was the alarm that sounded a keep clear alert?

She took a deep breath and pulled the door open.

A cursory glance found still, unmarked bodies slumped where they'd fallen. She didn't notice any countdowns or screen displays that suggested she'd only a few seconds to do something sensational before the station self-destructed.

She relaxed a little. All she had to do now was find the communications desk and get a message out.

Walking through the desks, she pushed and pulled bodies away from the terminals here and there until she found the one she needed. She set her rifle on the desk, pushed the body from its chair and sat down.

As expected, the computer was locked, but she forced a restart.

Drumming her fingers on the desk, willing it to go faster.

She leaned forward and was monetarily stunned by a heavy blow to the back of her neck, smacking her head on the desk.

Rolling off the chair, she looked up to see a figure in an environmental suit going for the rifle.

It wasn't her intention to get this far to be disabled before she could get the message out.

Struggling to make her eyes focus and get her brain to kick back in, she tried to generate an influence that would suggest to the figure that the gun was going to be more of a hindrance than a help.

She was successful in that the jerk turned its attention back to her, but that meant it was trying to kill her where she lay.

A mixed blessing.

Flailing about on the floor, she was trying to regain her footing, press an attack, and continue to generate a useful influence.

As the adrenaline kicked in, so did her training, and she could get to her feet and more effectively parry the undisciplined blows of her opponent.

Time seemed to slow down, and in the gaps between the seconds, Cora influenced the level of panic in her opponent so that it became more confused and less coordinated.

As it lost its ability to mount an effective defence, she influenced further, to reduce its confidence in itself.

It was enough to give her the break she needed to force it backwards, grab the rifle and fire.

It was outraged, and came at her with renewed vigour and a loud roar, so she fired again and again, emptying the magazine into it.

She backed away as it kept coming, pulling out the spent magazine and dropping it on the floor as she pulled a replacement from her pocket.

As she was shoving the new magazine into place, her opponent slipped on the spent one and crashed into the desk, sending computer equipment flying everywhere.

It rolled off the desk and lay still on the floor.

She hoped that 30 bullets were enough to keep it down, but backed further away, trying to work out how she'd stupidly missed someone in an environmental suit during her initial inspection of the room.

A glance around the room revealed that part of the wall was, in fact, a concealed door, still ajar, so she ducked low and skirted the edges of the control room until she got there.

It was the Director's office, and it was a mess.

The desk and chair overturned, papers and computer equipment strewn around the room as if a madman had turned the place over in some kind of fit.

More significantly, the Director was not in it.
Was it the Director who'd attacked her?
And why was he wearing an environmental suit?
Was he the one who'd attacked the station?
But why?

She returned to the control room, half expecting the body in the suit to have disappeared, but it lay where she'd left it.

In an attractively spreading pool of blood.

After hefting it with a solid kick to be sure it was dead, she pulled the suit helmet off to find it was the Director, his eyes wide, with dilated pupils. A smear of blood had dried below his nostrils.

What the fuck?

Was he a rebel or something?

At that point, she almost gave up, but despite everything, she needed to contact the Director General's office.

Apart from all other concerns, she needed to eat, and there was no telling what might be safe.

She sighed and rubbed the back of her neck where the Director had hit her.

Reluctantly putting down her rifle again, she picked up the bits of computer equipment and plugged them back together.

She'd never influenced technology before, but she closed her eyes and placed both hands near the equipment, telling it to work. Then she took a deep breath and pushed the on button.

It whirred compliantly.

While she'd made it this far, Cora still knew nothing more than the most general of basic security protocols, so that was what she'd have to use.

Crossing her fingers, she logged into the Directorate network and pinged the Director General's office, requesting a secure channel. Hopefully, the Exploratorem initiation code would be sufficient for her to be shunted through to someone who could help.

The adrenalin was wearing off, and the stress of the day was catching up with her. She was suddenly exhausted. She found her head bobbing as she dozed off, woken by a voice from the computer, "Attention Second Lieutenant Meadows."

Her head snapped upright as she surged out of the chair to attention.

"At ease Lieutenant."

She resumed her seat.

"What is the situation Meadows."

Not game to take the re-breather off. Cora pointed at it and quickly typed her response, "everyone dead

"director tried to halt comms

"had to kill."

"One moment please," the officer at the other end said.

Tinny music came through the speaker as the screen dissolved into a swirl of colour, pulsating in time with the music.

Cora leaned back in her chair, stretching.

A burst of static and she was face-to-face with General Bruce. She remained seated, but saluted.

"Well done Meadows.

"My adjutant is organising a relief mission. We're sending choppers in. You'll have help by dinnertime."

She nodded once.

"You'll start hearing some noises as we take control of the environmental and security systems from here, but I assure you, you'll be perfectly safe."

She nodded again.

A cool breeze caressed her face, and she typed "air moving now."

"Good. Your re-breather may be compromised, so please keep it on until you get outside."

Cora nodded once.

"I know it's not your speciality, but do you have any theories about the cause of the deaths? It will help the incoming troops decide where to start."

She started typing again, in full sentences given who she was "talking" to, "the dead include rodents, station personnel and at least one sentry outside. The Director was wearing an environmental suit. Perhaps chemical or EM pulse."

"I'll pass that along."

"Thank you sir."

"In the meantime, wait outside for the relief troops to arrive."

"Thank you sir."

The General looked towards someone sitting on his left, nodded once and turned his attention back to her.

"We have control of the situation now. You are dismissed."

She nodded and saluted. The General returned the salute, and the Security Directorate screen saver appeared on the screen.

Taking the rifle with her, she left the station, removed the re-breather and returned to the fields.

She'd snack on some fruit, and take a nap while she waited.

THE END

ALEXANDRIA
BLAELOCK
AUTHOR OF FATE IN YOUR HANDS
PURSUIT
OF
POWER
A SECURITY DIRECTORATE SHORT STORY

PURSUIT OF POWER

It was a beautiful afternoon.

The sunlight glinted off the glass windows of the executive residential towers at exactly the right angle to blind anyone dumb enough to enter its hallowed sanctum.

The tall trees provided a canopy that protected the internal parkland area and koi pond from the heat, and the rhododendron shrubbery deflected the wind at ground level.

Rustic paved paths wended their way from corner to corner, providing secluded, private nooks for whatever the rich bastards got up to when no one was looking.

Though she felt sorry for the foreign maid who'd found her mistress's dead body sprawled by the pond.

Captain Tara Cline scowled at the dead woman at her feet. As soon as she'd rolled it over and seen its empty eye sockets, it was as much as she could do not to kick it.

"Well, well, well," came a voice from behind her, "if it isn't Captain Conjecture."

She closed her eyes and turned her face to the sun for a moment, before sighing and turning with a flick of her navy-blue uniform greatcoat.

Clicking her heels together, she nodded at him, "Captain Reprehensible. I wish I could say it was a pleasure to see you again."

Unfortunately, it was a pleasure to see his body; tall and slim, his uniform subtly tailored to enhance his physical attributes.

But for fuck's sake, when he opened his mouth and started talking, she just wanted to pull out her side arm and shoot him in the face.

He grinned, revealing neat and even straight white teeth.

"Then no doubt you'll be delighted to know that after eight eyeless corpses, I've been reassigned to assist you with your enquiries."

That was all she needed, the popular and well-connected Captain Max Wade hanging around and getting in the way.

Both Eugenics Programme successes, they'd passed Genomics Bureau post-natal testing around the same time. Attended, competed, and survived the State Academy of Cultural Regulation together, each with a useful genetic "superpower."

Back at the University of Civilisation, they'd dated for a nanosecond, during which she'd discovered his genetic "superpower" was the ability to get information out of people.

When he'd used it to discover hers was the ability to read what people saw in the last moments of their lives.

Through their cold, dead, sightless eyes.

And then he'd dumped her, presumably for someone with a power more advantageous to his long-term career and social position.

Not that the University permitted unsanctioned relationships, but you get up to a lot of stupid stuff at university.

And why bother asking for permission when you've no intention of making it last?

Despite the obvious suitability of their postings, it had irritated her to hear at the announcement ceremony they were both allocated to Investigations. Though happily, she hadn't seen hide nor hair of him in the last few years.

Only heard on the grapevine of his astronomical case closure rate.

She held out her hand, wiggling her fingers. "Orders please."

He held out the paper, but when she tried to pull it from his hand, he didn't let go.

Frowning, she met his eyes, and well aware that breaking his stare would seem like a sign of weakness, she gazed steadily at him.

After a few seconds, she felt him release his grip slightly and snatched the paper from his hands.

With an almost imperceptible winner's smile, she unfolded it to confirm what he'd said.

At eight dead, the bodies of Security Directorate officers were piling up. The lack of eyeballs to read was an inconvenience, but did Wade's appointment mean the Investigator General doubted her competence?

She refolded the paper precisely and tucked it in the breast pocket of her uniform jacket.

"I am ecstatic," she said, ramming her balled fists into her coat pockets, "with the official Directorate busybody on the case, I'm sure we'll wrap this nonsense up in no time at all."

He clutched his heart with two hands and staggered back a couple of steps. "I'm heartbroken you'd say such a thing. Especially when anyone can *see* you so clearly need my help."

Tara turned her back on him, and marched across to her investigations team and issued instructions, "the usual. Lieutenant Valdes; take the maid's statement, cordon off the area, do a local door knock for witnesses, and get the coroner's office and crime scene out."

Valdes nodded.

Max caught up and threw an arm around her shoulders, "so, Cline, what's the goss?"

Tara clenched her teeth. He'd been here less than five minutes, and already he was trying to undermine her credibility with her team.

Turning to face him, she twisted out from under his arm, without breaking it, much as she'd have liked to, and gestured at her lieutenant. "Captain Wade, this is Lieutenant Valdes. Valdes, Captain Wade is joining our investigation team today."

Valdes clicked his heels together and nodded before offering his hand, "Welcome to the team Captain Wade, I've heard a lot about you."

Max shook the offered hand and clapped Valdes on the shoulder, "as have I of you."

Valdes took on the look of a puppy blessed by a hearty, leg jerking belly rub. "I look forward to working with you. Can I show you the crime scene?"

Wade glanced at her. Somehow she managed an impassive face, and he nodded and allowed himself to be led away by the lieutenant.

She let her body relax a fraction, leaned on the nearby ruin of a shrine and pretended to leaf through her notebook while she thought through the implications of his appointment to her team.

At least she was still nominally in charge of the task force, which meant he was her resource, to do with what she thought was best.

Given the choice, he certainly wasn't the person she would've asked for, but his impressive case closure rate wasn't solely because of his interrogative powers.

He had a keen analytic mind, and she wasn't so petty as to send such a valuable resource packing when a fresh perspective might be useful.

A slight throat-clearing made her aware they had returned.

"Right. Valdes," she said, pocketing the notebook, "I'll take Captain Wade back to the office and bring him up to speed on the investigations so far. Let me know what you find."

He nodded in reply, "Ma'am."

And then to Max, "Sir."

And the sooner they got these cases solved, the sooner he'd be the hell out of her sight.

«« • »»

Back in the crowded, messy incident room, the first step was to knock on Major Kron's door to introduce Captain Wade and pass the orders on.

Naturally, the fat and lazy Kron needed a bit of time to fawn over the Superstar investigator.

She closed the door and left them to it. She'd already seen enough male bonding to last a lifetime.

She hung up her coat and cap as she returned to her desk, fortunately at the back of the room with five desks between her and Kron's Office, though sadly still facing it. On more than one occasion, she'd suddenly felt uncomfortable and looked up to see him staring at her in a way she couldn't interpret, but made her skin crawl nonetheless.

She logged into her computer, updated the initial victim and location details, and restarted the search for potential links. Then she printed pictures of the victim, dead and alive, as well as some of the scene.

With that out of the way, she lined up a new blank board alongside the other seven on the opposite wall, stuck the pictures to it and wrote out the pertinent victim details.

At this rate, she'd need to put the Supply Department on her speed dial.

The latest victim was a general's wife, so at least she wouldn't be required to carry out the Death Knock. That would be the Major's responsibility.

Ordinarily, she'd attend to observe the spouse's reaction, but this would be an excellent opportunity to put Wade to immediate use and get him out of her way.

The investigation would likely proceed on the assumption the General was innocent anyway, especially as his wife's appointment within the Directorate seemed in keeping with the context of the other murders.

Standing back far enough to see all the boards at once, she crossed her arms and tried to get her thoughts in enough of a semblance of order to brief Wade.

So far, all they'd identified was that the victims were Security Directorate officers, with no obvious defence wounds, and of course, the missing eyeballs.

No common appointments, ranks, genders, powers, location of work or motive.

No common *modus operandi* either, though it looked like the killer had targeted each victim in such a way they'd couldn't defend themselves.

And they'd scooped the eyeballs out with surgical precision, *post mortem*.

Of course, it was probably easier to remove the eyeballs after death (suggesting a single killer), but not for the first time, she wondered why the murderer didn't take them out first to disable the victim.

What did the killer hope to achieve from that?

Was it just a way to stop her from doing her thing?

Or a way to attract her attention and suspicion, to send the investigation into a dead end?

"Have you considered that the order of the murders is significant?" Wade startled her by asking.

She looked at him sharply, expecting mockery, but he was looking at the boards with his hands tucked casually in his trouser pockets.

"Why would I?"

"Ah, I guess you haven't needed to know before."

She frowned and made an impatient gesture. "What?"

"You know that rumour about how you can steal someone's powers if you kill them?"

She nodded her head sharply once.

"Under certain circumstances, it's true."

Tara growled with frustration, "I've got seven, I mean eight dead Directive officers and no one thought to share this with me?"

He shrugged, "perhaps as you should have been informed by now, they thought you knew."

"And that's something Kron should have passed on?"

"He's the most likely source, though it's possible he doesn't know either."

"How could they could promote you to Major and not know this?"

Wade said nothing, just looked at the floor and scrubbed at a mark on it with his toe.

"I see," she looked up at the ceiling, willing the tears of frustration away, "and now you swan in and solve the case in five minutes flat."

The ghost of a smile crossed his face. "I know I'm good, but I'm not that good."

"And what else is there that you're not telling me? You have a suspect, and it's someone highly placed."

Again, he avoided her eyes and didn't reply.

"This fucking day just gets better and better."

"Could be worse though. You're still in charge."

She snorted, "yeah, but for how long?"

"This case, at the very least."

"So, I've got eight murders to solve before the high-ranking killer strikes again."

"So now you're aware of the stakes. Let's get investigating."

She glanced at him, but couldn't detect any malicious intent.

"Fine," she gestured at the conference table in the centre of the incident room, "let's sit down and work this through.

"Aside from Officer status in the Directorate, we haven't identified any commonalities that suggest a reason these people were targeted."

She grabbed a bunch of files from her desk and tossed them on the table in front of him. He reached out to stop them from sliding off the other side.

"Am I authorised to share your new information with the team?"

He looked at her for a long moment, "if you think it would help the investigation."

She paced a few laps around the table while he flicked through the files and sorted them into the order of killing.

"Okay," walking past the boards, she picked up a marker and stopped beside the first, "let's not worry about sharing that detail right now, let's just focus on what the path of powers reveals. This is the first victim, Private Holly Devine. What's her power?"

"Find missing items."

"Right, the body in the library." Tara wrote that on the board and moved to the next, "victim two, Major Steven Smith.

"Power to manipulate metals."

"OK, Jewellery workshop. Next, victim three, Lieutenant John Peterson."

"Open doors."

Smiling, she snorted, "women's dorm."

He laughed, then she remembered they weren't friends and turned away.

"Private Sam Marlowe."

"Disrupt electronic communications."

"Propaganda Bureau studios. Then Captain Mike Colquhoun."

"Super strength."

"The gym. Followed by Private Jane Cooper."

"Levitation."

"Highpoint Tower. Next, Captain James Dalgleish."

"Setting fire."

"Local pool. And now we've Lieutenant Colonel Jennifer Frank."

"Melding glass."

"Astronomy lab."

They looked at each other, grinning.

Tara asked, "put it together, and what have you got?"

"Thief!" they said in unison.

Max held his hand up, and before she could stop herself, she'd slapped it.

Remembering he was probably after her job, she stepped back, turned away and looked again at the boards.

"So, if you're trying to become a better thief, what are you stealing, and what other powers are you going to need?"

He came to stand behind her, looking at the boards. "Something you have to find, get into a room with, that's so heavy you need help to move it, and then cover your traces."

She could almost feel his chest moving as he breathed, but the only way to break away from him was through him.

She turned to look at him, "like something in a locked case in a museum or gallery? Some kind of artefact you thought would give you the power to do something you wouldn't otherwise be able to do?"

"Like what, take over the Directorate?"

She turned back to the boards to let the idea sink in. Wasn't it a bit farfetched to think someone might try to steal an artefact to overthrow the Directorate?

"Given that information about powers is strictly controlled, how does our killer know who to target to gain the right powers?"

"We don't..." Wade started, "they don't know yet, but I think we can assume the killer is authorised to access that information."

"But isn't access strictly controlled and monitored?"

"Yes."

"Is it possible they have a power that helps them conceal their actions?"

"I suppose. It's also possible they've killed previously, and for whatever reason, those murders haven't been linked."

She rubbed the back of her neck, "so we should probably pull the files of all Directorate officer murders. But how far back?"

He shrugged one shoulder, "and how wide? When were you appointed to this task force, and on what basis?"

She frowned, "Wade, wouldn't it be easier to kill me than to keep scooping the eyeballs out?"

He just looked at her, expressionless.

"So not just another murder, but my own murder."

He nodded once in the affirmative.

"So, why are you really here?"

"Did you get a Notification of Union from the Bureau yet?"

"No, but I've been sleeping in the barracks lately, and haven't been home. How exactly is that relevant?"

He offered her a copy of an order from the Genomics Bureau.

Which announced the Directorate eugenics programme had done whatever it was it did, and paired her with him for a five-year contract. Dated June 15, with 21 days for appeal, all over and done with already.

Annoying.

Partly because she just didn't have time for a Union, and partly because it was him in particular.

She screwed up the paper and, as much as she wanted to drop-kick it into a nearby wastepaper basket, just let it fall to the floor as she turned on her heel, collected her hat and coat, and left the incident room.

«« • »»

Filled with murderous rage towards Wade, she paced the night streets silently, daring someone to attack her.

Though of course, only an insane person with a death wish was going to attack a uniformed Security Directorate Captain.

The longer she walked, the angrier she got, and the less of a bead she could get on someone trying to take over the Directorate.

After a point, she just wanted to kill something or someone and broke into the old barracks gym. Not that she didn't have easy access using the security code, but sometimes you needed to test your other skills.

Despite its scruffiness, she much preferred it to the new one, which was mainly inhabited by show-offs and poseurs, not people working seriously to maintain combat readiness.

How some people kept their postings was beyond her.

The old one, with its blood-stained walls and scratched up wood floor, was for serious work.

She threw her coat and hat aside, rolled up her sleeves, and wound some abandoned tape from the floor around her hands.

Then launched herself at a punching bag.

The air was acrid with stale sweat, and she had to keep tossing her head to stop her own from dripping in her eyes.

The sound of each blow echoed across the empty workout space and back again. She half expected the human-shaped punching bag to kneel and beg her to stop hitting it.

Maybe that was why someone else had pasted a cross shaped adhesive tape bandage on its head.

Having worked the first layer of brutal rage out of her system, she tried to think more logically about the murders, but Wade and her impending nuptials just kept getting in the way.

Perhaps she should give herself a break, towel down her face, drink some water and bloody try harder.

She unwound the tapes from her hands and grimaced at the bruises coming to the surface. Too late to put them back on. Her knuckles were already swelling.

Just one more annoyance in a day of nothing but annoyances.

She walked across to the water fountain, rinsed her mouth out and spat on the floor.

Given the pain in her jaw, she now knew she'd been clenching her teeth as well.

Bloody hell!

It'd only taken a couple of hours with him to stress her almost to breaking point.

Of all people, why did it have to be fucking Captain Max Wade?

Not that it was about him, or her, but the Directorate's breeding program.

Sometimes, the matches were so successful the parties renewed their contracts or even applied for permanence.

Though whether that was something to be envied was hard to know.

Did he request the Union, or was he really allocated by a random genetic match as the programme claimed?

Was it possible the Union was a way to provide 24-hour protection to an at-risk officer?

Was the Union even real?

Should she go home and check?

Mind you, he'd implied a senior officer could be responsible for the killings, so it was possible he was investigating her.

Or was he investigating higher up her chain?

His orders had seemed genuine, but where had he come from?

As she came to a halt, she realised she'd been pacing the floor.

Who did she know outside her chain who could discreetly check on that?

Alumni Association?

It had been less than a day since the transfer orders had been served, they wouldn't know to update their records yet, would they?

She did a quick circuit of the gym to make sure she really was alone, then broke into the office to use the phone. She flicked through the phone book until she found the listing and called the number.

It rang and rang and rang.

And just as she realised how late it was, and decided to hang up, someone answered the phone.

She spouted some nonsense about needing to contact him and received confirmation of her suspicions.

Bureau of Internal Investigations.

She hung up the phone, removed the evidence of her break and enter, and relocked the door as she left.

So, Wade was an II agent. Though that didn't get her any closer to knowing who was under investigation.

Or whether she could trust him.

She spun on one heel and launched a sidekick at the dummy.

It rocked back and forth on its stand, but didn't fight back.

Because it was immobile.

The missing piece of the puzzle!

The murderer could immobilise the victims. Before they knew they needed to fight back. And with the other stolen powers, it could be a man or woman.

Who could do whatever they wanted to because the victims couldn't fight back.

So Wade had helped her enquiries after all.

And now she had to tell him so he could cross-check his suspects.

She turned to walk away, but tripped over her feet and fell to the floor instead.

It wasn't until she tried to stand up she realised she couldn't move.

She tried again, harder, but remained uncomfortably prone on the floor.

"There's no point trying to move my dear Captain Cline, I have you pinned like a bug.

In fact, I think I might squash you like one too. I haven't done that before, and I think it might be fun."

She heard Major Kron laugh, and even worse, it sounded like he'd slapped his leg at his own joke.

How ridiculously melodramatic.

She couldn't even open her mouth to denounce him.

Couldn't even growl her frustration.

In any case, with the sensation of increasing weight on her back, it was getting harder to breathe, let alone speak.

"I was planning to let you live and take the fall, but once Wade arrived, I knew it wouldn't take the two of you long to figure out I've been withholding information crucial to the investigations."

If she could have grunted, she would, though a power kick to the balls would have disabled him momentarily as well as shut him the fuck up.

Not that Kron had ever seemed that competent, but then again, his role was more along the lines of managing the officers, their training, equipment, and welfare.

Not actually hands-on investigation.

As she gasped for air, she wondered for the first time how he'd achieved his command.

Did it involve another power he'd stolen from someone else?

Dammit, there were still so many questions, and it was looking like she wasn't going to get any answers.

Except with her senses on high alert, she thought she heard the faintest scrape of a service boot from one of the room's darkened corners.

Leaping to the conclusion someone was coming to her aid, she willed herself to stop fighting and relax enough to get a good spring when Kron's attention shifted.

Except, of course, the weight on her back was increasing, and as she relaxed, she felt several sharp pains in her chest signalling broken ribs.

She couldn't breathe, she couldn't move, she couldn't think.

She passed out.

«« • »»

She woke in pain, who knows how much later.

The white room was too bright, too cold, and smelled too strongly of an alcoholic antiseptic.

The hum of air conditioning and beeping machines was disorienting as well as deafening.

Her head hurt, her body hurt, and she was incredibly thirsty.

She groaned.

Almost instantly, someone beside her took her hand, and shortly after, she passed out again.

When she woke, the pain was almost bearable, the light dimmer and the air conditioner quieter. She could hear voices murmuring nearby.

Propped on a pile of pillows, she was more or less comfortable.

But still thirsty.

She tried to move her hand to the call button, but someone was holding it. In both of his hands, resting his head on them.

She tugged her hand. He didn't let go, but raised his tousled head to reveal Wade's bloodshot eyes. Along with his torn and bloodstained uniform shirt.

He looked at her silently for a moment, and she resisted the temptation to smooth down his hair.

He set her hand down on the crisp bed covers, picked up a glass of water from the table, adjusted the straw and brought it to her mouth to drink.

Water had never tasted so good.

She sipped and sipped, but when she tried to breathe at the same time, she started coughing, and the pain of it almost stopped her breathing altogether.

Wade quickly took her hand again, and the pain receded along with the need to cough.

Which was confusing, because his power was being a truth serum, so he shouldn't be able to take the pain away.

Except he'd mentioned when you killed a Directorate officer, it was possible to take their powers...

She wondered vaguely how many people he'd killed.

And that led to further speculation about how the powers stacked up, whether they ever cancelled each other out, if you could give them away or otherwise divest them.

And as she drifted back to sleep, whether this power was analgesic or anaesthetic.

The next time she woke, she was blessedly alone, with a call button in her hand.

She pushed the button.

A moment later, a pretty nurse bustled in, used a small torch to look into her eyes before taking her blood pressure, pulse, and temperature.

Tara let her complete her observations before asking, "how long have I been here?"

"Not long, only a couple of days."

A couple of days! There was too much to do to be out of contact for a couple of days.

"And when can I leave?"

"I'm afraid I can't tell you that, but I've paged the doctor, and he'll be along shortly."

Tara wanted to know exactly what was going on, but it seemed the nurse couldn't help her.

There was no point in getting agitated. That wouldn't get her answers any quicker, so she only nodded and let the nurse leave.

The next person she saw was a clean and starched Wade, in full uniform with new Major pips on his epaulettes.

She opened her mouth to make a sarcastic comment but, remembering he sat by her bed in blood-stained clothing, holding her hand, closed it after saying nothing.

Not to mention the impending union...

He tossed his peaked cap onto the table, hooked a chair closer with his foot and sat next to the bed, looking at her for what seemed like a long time.

"I assume you'd like an update?"

She nodded.

"The Academy initially assessed William Kron as a low-level generalist, but redirected him to specialist training after he showed some signs of talent. We now know he killed his first officer cadet and took her power during this time."

She nodded again.

"Despite his apparent laziness and lack of class attendance, he graduated from University with Honours. We've since tied him back to several other murders during this time."

She smiled tightly, so she wasn't the only one who'd noticed his general lack of ability.

"He progressed rapidly through the ranks, applying for and receiving promotional transfers around the time his superiors suspected his abilities weren't as exceptional as he'd portrayed them. And more than one colonel was happier to pass him on than to start disciplinary procedures."

She shook her head in disbelief.

"However, his last colonel notified Internal Investigations. We seeded the rumour of a mind-controlling ancient artefact, and we've been monitoring him closely since then."

"How was he able to kill so many officers while you were watching him?"

"We weren't aware of the extent of his murder spree until just recently. We classified several of the killings as accidental deaths, so we weren't tracking those powers."

"And by just recently, you mean until you killed him."

He looked at the floor but didn't deny it.

"So, since his first days at school, he more or less built up a massive grievance against the Directorate and decided he had to control it."

"Or perhaps even earlier, his parents signed him over to the State after their attempt to abort the foetus failed."

"I suppose some normals don't take it so well when they find they're carrying "superheroes"."

"No."

"So how do I come into the story?"

"We're not sure how you came to his attention, perhaps your ambition and exemplary service record. But we think at least some of his recent murders were intended to trigger the creation of a task force and get you assigned to it."

She shuddered as she grunted, and when the pain hit, sat up and grabbed her stomach.

He leaned across the bed, took one of her hands, and the pain receded.

So much better, "thanks for that."

She unsuccessfully attempted to withdraw her hand. "Um, how many powers do you have?"

"32."

"Are they all Kron's?"

"No."

"I see. And how long have you been licensed to kill Directorate officers?"

"I can't say."

She leaned back on her pillows and tried again to withdraw her hand.

"So. They assigned you to the task force to protect me, the Union was cover for staying close, and now you'll be moving on to another assignment?"

He laughed, "I'm not sorry to say that the Union is real, though it's postponed until you're up and about again."

She inspected him closely.

Just like her, he was a little older, maybe a little more mature. The creep of grey across his temples gave him a distinguished look.

He looked worried, and she tried not to smile.

"Stop," he said, you're embarrassing me."

They'd had some fun at Uni, and she really could do a lot worse than a Union with him.

Tara still wasn't entirely sure she was happy about the Union, but after another unsuccessful attempt to extract her hand, decided she objected slightly less.

THE END

ABOUT THE AUTHOR

Alexandria Blaelock writes stories, some of them for *Ellery Queen's Mystery Magazine* and *Pulphouse Fiction Magazine*.

She's also written five self-help books applying business techniques to personal matters like getting dressed, cleaning house, and feeding your friends.

She lives in a forest because she enjoys birdsong, the scent of gum leaves and the sun on her face. When not telecommuting to parallel universes from her Melbourne based imagination, she watches K-dramas, talks to animals, and drinks Campari. At the same time.

Discover more at www.alexandriablaelock.com.

... or the collections

... or *The Ghost and Ms Cox*

Life interrupted

To say the letter was a surprise was an understatement. It arrived addressed to Miss Finlay Cox, which made the contents even more extraordinary.

Orphan Finn Cox inherits a cottage. Thinks it holds the key to her origins. Of course she takes a look. Who wouldn't?

But when she gets there, she gets more than she bargained for.

Is it friend, family or foe?

www.ingramcontent.com/pod-product-compliance
Lightning Source LLC
Chambersburg PA
CBHW031254210726